Buster's Naughty Tricks

This book belongs to

daisy Joyner

have a nice read !!!

STRIPES PUBLISHING
An imprint of Magi Publications
1 The Coda Centre, 189 Munster Road,
London SW6 6AW

A paperback original
First published in Great Britain in 2011

Text copyright © Sue Mongredien, 2011
Illustrations copyright © Artful Doodlers, 2011
Photographs copyright © iStockphoto.com, 2011

ISBN: 978-1-84715-169-8

The right of Sue Mongredien and Artful Doodlers to be
identified as the author and illustrator of this work
respectively has been asserted by them in accordance
with the Copyright, Designs and Patents Act, 1988.

A CIP catalogue record for this book is available
from the British Library.

Printed and bound in the UK.

10 9 8 7 6 5 4 3 2 1

Sue Mongredien

Kitten Club

Buster's Naughty Tricks

stripes

Meet the Kitten Club girls!

Amy
& Ginger

Mia
& Smokey

Molly
& Truffle

Ella
& Honey

Ruby
& Ziggy

Lily
& Buster

Chapter I

"Lily! Are you ready? We need to leave for Kitten Club in two minutes!"

Lily McCarthy jumped at the sound of her mum's voice. Oops! She'd completely lost track of time, practising her audition piece in her bedroom. The school play was being cast on Monday and Lily was desperate to get the best part.

"Coming!" she shouted. "I'll just say goodbye to Buster."

Buster was Lily's black kitten. He was nearly five months old and absolutely adorable, but also rather naughty. He liked sharpening his claws on the furniture, and jumping up on to the kitchen worktops, where he wasn't allowed. He also had the bad habit of curling up and going to sleep in the worst possible places … like on Mum's best silk pyjamas, or on the television with his tail dangling over the screen. The other day he'd even dozed off in the fruit bowl, leaving black fur all over the apples.

"Buster," Lily called, "where are you?"

She heard a sleepy meow from Mum and Dad's bedroom and her heart sank. Oh dear. Buster wasn't supposed to go in there since

he'd made holes in Mum's favourite pyjamas.
She hurried in and scanned the room. Bed,
wardrobe, chest of drawers, baby Jessica's
cot… Uh-oh. Buster was in Jessica's cot,
snuggled up with her pink teddy, and
looking very pleased with himself.

"Buster!" Lily hissed. "What are you
doing in there?"

"Lily, we need to go," her mum called from downstairs.

"One minute!" she yelled back. She reached an arm into the cot and quickly scooped up her kitten. He began rumbling with purrs, but Lily didn't feel quite so happy. There was black fur all over Jessica's sheet and baby sleeping bag. Mum was going to go mad!

"Oh, Buster," she said, taking him out of the room and shutting the door firmly behind her. "What am I going to do with you?"

Mum wasn't too pleased to hear about Buster's latest sleeping place when Lily broke the news in the car on the way to Kitten Club.

"How did he get in there?" Mum said
crossly. "I know I didn't leave the door
open."

Lily swallowed, remembering how she'd
gone in the bedroom earlier to borrow
Mum's hairbrush. "I … I think I might
have left it open," she said. "Sorry, Mum."

Her mum sighed as she parked outside
Mia's house and turned off the engine.
"We'll just have to keep a closer eye on

what he's doing, and where he is," she said, unclipping her seat belt. "And we'll have to try extra hard to remember to keep bedroom doors shut, so that he can't sneak in, OK?"

Mum got out and walked round to open the car door for Lily. She looked tired, Lily thought, noticing the dark rings under her eyes. She knew her mum hadn't slept very well lately because Jessica had been cutting a new tooth and had been crying a lot in the night. To make matters worse, Dad was working in Scotland for a few weeks, so he wasn't around to help out.

Lily got out of the car and gave her mum a hug. "Sorry," she said again. "I'll try harder to stop Buster from sleeping where he shouldn't, Mum, I promise."

Her mum hugged her back. "We'll both try," she said. "Have fun at Kitten Club, love. Molly's mum's going to pick you up, OK?"

Lily waved as her mum drove away, then walked quickly through the rain up to Mia's front door. She knew her friends would be sympathetic about Buster's tricks at least. Thank goodness for Kitten Club!

Chapter 2

"Hi, Lily," Mia said, letting her inside. "Great news. Dad's taken my sisters out to visit my aunty, so it's just us lot and Mum. Result!"

"Yay!" said Lily, stepping into the warm house. Mia had one older sister and one younger and neither of them was very good at letting the Kitten Club girls have their meetings in peace.

Lily followed Mia into the living room where the other girls were already waiting. There were six of them in Kitten Club altogether – Lily, Mia, Molly, Ella, Amy and Ruby. Their kittens were all brothers and sisters, and the girls had met when they'd chosen them at Chestnut Farm in the summer.

"Hi, guys," Lily said as she walked into the room. "And hello, Smokey," she added, seeing Mia's fluffy grey kitten curled up on Amy's lap.

"Hi, Lily," the others chorused, smiling back at her.

"How's Buster?" asked Molly.

Lily groaned theatrically and shook her head. "Gorgeous but naughty," she said.

"I had to turf him out of Jessica's cot just now. I thought Mum was going to crash the car, she was so cross when I told her where I'd found him."

"Oops," Ruby said. "Ziggy fell asleep on one of my teddies yesterday. They looked so cute – as if they were having a cuddle!"

Mia and Lily sat down with the others, then Mia opened up the Kitten Club scrapbook, which the girls filled in every week, and turned to the next free page. "Now that we're all here, let's do the roll-call," she said. "Green-Eyes?"

"Meow," Amy said, answering to her club name.

"Moggy?"

"Meow," said Molly.

"Glamour-Puss?"

"Meow," said Ruby.

"Scatty?"

"Meow … prrrr," said Lily, rubbing her head against Ella's arm, just like a cat. Everybody giggled.

"Tomboy?"

"M-Meow," Ella managed to get out, still laughing.

"And Witch-Cat, that's me," Mia said, ticking herself off.

"I've got something for you all," Amy said when Mia had finished. She reached into a plastic bag next to her and pulled out a sheaf of paper. "It's our magazine – Mum printed copies for everyone!"

The other girls let out loud squeals of excitement, making Smokey jerk awake, his ears swivelling back in surprise. Then his eyes widened happily at the sight of the empty plastic bag on the floor and he stood up, wiggled his bottom and pounced on it.

The girls all roared with laughter as the bag
– and Smokey – went skidding along the
carpet. He gave a mew of alarm and leaped
off, staring suspiciously at the bag.

"Oh, Smokey," Mia giggled. "You
looked like you were sledging then. Are you
practising in case it snows?"

"Dad said today's weather forecast is for
snow," Amy said excitedly. "I hope they're
right! Anyway," she went on, handing out
copies of *MEOW!*, the special Kitten Club
magazine that they'd made. "Have a look
at these!"

Her friends opened their copies at once.
They'd each contributed different things to
the magazine – jokes, puzzles, news and all
sorts of other fun stuff.

"Oh, wow," Molly said, leafing through

her copy. "It looks awesome. I'm going to keep this forever."

"I can't wait to show Ziggy that he's in print." Ruby smiled, turning to a page she'd written about her kitten, which included a photo of him. "Fame at last!"

"We've got to do another copy in the new year," Mia said happily, scooping Smokey on to her lap as she read. "This looks fab."

Once everyone had admired the magazine, the girls took it in turns to share their news. "We're getting our Christmas tree tomorrow," Ella said, hugging her knees. "I can't wait. Although I'm wondering what Honey's going to think of it. She's probably going to climb up it, knowing her."

"I bet Buster will do the same," Lily said, rolling her eyes. "Can you imagine how excited the kittens will be with all those baubles swinging from the branches? Buster will think it's an enormous toy, just for him."

"What are you getting your kittens for Christmas?" Amy asked. "I saw a really cute feeding bowl in town with paw-prints painted round it. I'm saving up my pocket money to buy it for Ginger."

"I might get Truffle a red velvet collar," Molly said thoughtfully. "She'd look so smart in it – and Christmassy too!"

"Ziggy's going to have smoked haddock for his Christmas dinner," Ruby said. "It's his absolute favourite treat."

Mia glanced at Smokey, who had leaped off her lap and was chasing a marble across the room. "We don't celebrate Christmas, but I'm going to get Smokey a present anyway," she said. "Have you seen those toy hamsters that whizz around everywhere? He would love one of those to play with."

Mia's mum came into the room just then. "Girls, would you like to make cookies?" she asked. "I've got some special cookie cutters that I thought you might like…" She held up two silver cutters – one shaped like a cat's head, and one the shape of a cat sitting up.

"Yes, please!" Amy cried, getting to her feet at once.

"Ooh, yummy," the others echoed.

"Go and wash your hands, then, and meet me in the kitchen." Mia's mum smiled.

The girls didn't need telling twice! Mia's mum helped them make special cardamom cookie dough, then they took it in turns to roll out a lump of it and cut it into cat shapes.

While the cookies were baking, they washed up together. Mia scooped up some of the bubbles from the washing-up bowl and blew them into the air for Smokey to chase. As Lily dried the cutters, she told her friends about the school play she was planning to audition for. "It's called *The Christmas Angel*," she told them, and grinned. "Guess which part I'm hoping to get?"

"Could it be the Christmas Angel, by any chance?" Molly laughed.

"Got it in one," Lily said, high-fiving Molly. "I so hope they choose me. It's the best part in the whole show – and the best costume too. Sparkly wings and everything!" And then she was off, pretending to fly around the room, flapping her arms with a dreamy, angelic expression on her face.

"Si-i-i-ilent night," she warbled. "Ho-o-o-oly night…"

The others burst into laughter. Even Mrs Khaliq smiled at Lily's dramatics. "If anyone deserves to get the part, it's you, Lily," she said, taking a tray of sweet-smelling cookies from the oven. "But right now, I need you all to be kitchen angels and finish clearing up in here. Then, when these have cooled down, you can taste one. Do we have a deal?"

"Deal!" everyone chorused. Lily stopped flapping and smiled at her friends. She loved being in Kitten Club almost as much as she loved Christmas. And with Buster in the family now, she knew it was going to be the best Christmas ever.

Chapter 3

The next day, as soon as Lily woke up, she knew something was different. The light coming through the gap in her curtains looked strangely bright. She rolled out of bed – brrr, it was freezing – and pulled open the curtains … then squealed. It had snowed in the night, and the whole garden was covered in a thick white blanket!

"Mum! Mum!" she yelled, racing downstairs at full speed. "Have you seen the snow?"

Lily's mum was in the kitchen feeding Jessica her breakfast. Jessica bounced up and down in her high chair, beaming as her big sister burst into the room. "Yes, there's a lot, isn't there?" Mum said. "Have some breakfast, Lil, then we can wrap up warm and go outside."

Buster was sitting on the windowsill, staring out of the window with a puzzled expression, as if he didn't understand what had happened to his garden. Lily picked him up and danced around with him. "Oh, Buster, you're going to love the snow, it's so much fun! We can make a snowman, Mum. We can even make a snow-cat!"

Lily's mum laughed at her excitement. "Good idea," she said. "But how about breakfast first? There's porridge in the pan if you want something hot."

Buster didn't like being bounced around and squirmed out of Lily's arms, plopping down on to the table. Jessica shrieked in excitement as he skidded on the slippery surface. "Off the table, you!" Mum said to him, her smile vanishing. "Go on, shoo!"

Lily sat down with Buster on her lap, telling him all the fun things they were going to do in the snow, while she gobbled down her porridge. Then she went upstairs and put on three jumpers, a pair of leggings with tracksuit bottoms on top, and two pairs of socks, before coming down again to add her coat, a woolly hat, a scarf, gloves and her wellies.

"Ready!" she declared, waddling awkwardly to the back door. She was so bulky with all her layers that moving around felt very strange! "Come on, Buster, let's play outside. Snow is the best!"

Unfortunately, it quickly became clear that Buster didn't share Lily's view about snow being "the best". As soon as Lily plopped him down on the snowy ground, he gave a squeak of alarm and leaped on to her wellies, scrabbling up them in an attempt to keep his feet dry. "Oh, Buster," she giggled. "It's all right. It's fun! Try again."

She peeled his paws off her boots and set him down on the snow. Buster's legs still weren't very long, so the snow came right over his paws, and almost up to his soft tummy. He gazed up at Lily with big, bewildered eyes, as if to say, *Why are you doing this to me?*

Lily leaned down to stroke him. "It's OK, pickle," she said soothingly. "You'll get used to it. Come on, let's make footprints."

But Buster put his nose in the air and stalked off towards the back door. He'd had quite enough of the cold, thank you very much. He had to pick his feet up quite high to walk through the snow, leaving the cutest little prints. Bits of ice clung to his belly and he kept his tail firmly up as if he was determined not to get a single hair of it cold or wet.

Lily's mum came outside with Jessica balanced on her hip, and they watched Buster leap up the back step into the house and give himself a good shake. "He's as much of a drama queen as you are," Mum joked.

Lily felt a bit disappointed. "I wanted him to play with me, Mum," she said.

"Cats aren't very keen on snow," her mum said. "They don't like getting their paws wet."

"Oh well," Lily said. "Maybe he'll be a bit braver later on. Will you help me make a snow-cat, Mum? Let's make a really cute one." She grinned, seeing Buster watching them out of the window. "If we make a realistic-looking one, you never know, Buster might come out and try to make friends with it!"

"It was so much fun playing in the snow, Dad – I wish you'd been here with us," Lily said later that evening when he phoned.

"I wish I'd been there too," her dad

replied. "If it's still snowy when I'm back at Christmas we'll have the biggest and best snowball fight ever."

Lily smiled. She was curled up on the sofa in her pyjamas, having just got out of the bath, half watching Buster chasing a ball around while she chatted. "You will be back for the school play, won't you?" she asked. "The auditions are tomorrow and I'm going for the main part, you know."

"I'll do my best," Dad said, "but I can't promise anything at the moment."

Lily was distracted by Buster suddenly leaping on to the table and attacking a large pot plant. "I'd better go," she said, hurrying across the room as the cheeky kitten grabbed a dangling leaf with his paws and began swinging from it. "Bye, Dad."

"Good luck tomorrow," he said. "Bye, Lils."

"Buster!" Lily hissed, trying to detach his claws from the plant. He'd broken one of its stems so that it drooped down forlornly. "You're not allowed up here, you monkey," she told him, picking him up and kissing his nose. "Come upstairs with me instead. You can listen to me practise for my audition again."

The following morning, Lily felt jittery as she got ready for school. It was Auditions Day! She knew her words perfectly, but hoped her mind didn't go blank when it was her turn to perform. "I wish I could take you into school with me, Buster," she said as she finished brushing her teeth. "I need a lucky mascot today."

Buster, who was in the bathroom with her, seemed more interested in the long piece of toilet roll dangling from the holder than being a lucky mascot. He stretched up on his hind legs to pat it and almost fell over backwards. Lily giggled as she washed her face. Buster, meanwhile, was still desperate to reach the toilet roll.

He leaped up even higher this time, a paw outstretched, and managed to hook his claw into the paper. As he landed on the ground, the paper unrolled after him, falling in a heap on his head!

Lily burst out laughing as Buster gave a surprised squeak. He really was the funniest kitten in the world! "We'd better tidy this up before Mum notices," she said, still chuckling. "What a troublemaker!"

Buster gazed up at her, his beautiful green eyes wide and innocent-looking, as if to say, "Me? Trouble?"

Lily couldn't help giving him a cuddle before she tidied up. Troublemaker or not, she just couldn't resist him.

The auditions took place at lunchtime. As well as the part of the Christmas Angel, there were also roles for Mary, Joseph, three wise men, shepherds, a Christmas tree, a modern-day family and a whole host of other angels who'd be singing as a choir. Some of Lily's school friends were nervous about auditioning. Alice forgot her words and turned bright red. Willow looked terrified and couldn't manage more than a mumble. And Emily went all giggly and kept putting her hand over her mouth as if she was embarrassed. Watching them made Lily feel nervous too. She wanted to be the angel so badly!

When it was her turn to speak, she stood

up, took a deep breath, and tried to imagine
that she was the angel. She thought about
the graceful way an angel would move, and
tried to copy that grace as she walked to the
centre of the stage. She kept her head up,
looked straight at the teachers, then spoke
clearly and confidently.

As the words came out, she really felt for a moment that she was the Christmas Angel, and that she could make everyone in the world have the most wonderful Christmas. Before she knew it, she'd reached the end of her lines – and everybody clapped.

"Very nice, Lily, thank you," said Mrs Matthews, the drama teacher.

"You were awesome," Willow told her, her eyes shining, as she sat down again.

"You were fab," Emily agreed.

"Thank you," Lily said. It had taken her a few seconds to remember that she was Lily McCarthy, not the Christmas Angel after all. She crossed her fingers. "Let's hope the teachers thought so too."

Chapter 4

"Molly, it's Lily. Guess what?"

"What?" came Molly's voice down the phone.

"I got the part. I'm the Christmas Angel!"

"Oh, cool! Brilliant, Lily," Molly cried, sounding almost as excited as Lily felt.

Lily couldn't stop beaming. The cast

list had been put up at the end of the day
and she'd had to check it at least five
times before she could believe it was real.
But her name had been there in black and
white: Christmas Angel … Lily McCarthy.
YAY!

"I'm so chuffed," she told Molly. "It's
the biggest part by miles – I've got loads of
lines to learn." She stroked Buster, who was
climbing up her jumper and giggled as his
fluffy head tickled her neck. "The only bad
thing is that I've got rehearsals nearly every
night," she went on, trying to unhook
Buster's claws. "So I won't get to see Buster
so much after school. But it's only for a
few weeks."

"He'll be all right," Molly said. "Hey, will
your dad be back in time to see the show?"

Lily plopped Buster into her lap but he
scampered away and started
sharpening his claws on
the arm of the sofa.
"No, Buster!" she
yelped, as a thread
came loose. "Um … I
don't know," she replied
to Molly. "I hope so. He's
not sure yet. Anyway, just wanted to tell you
my good news. I'll see you on Saturday for
Kitten Club, OK? I'd better dash – Buster's
in one of his mad moods. Byeeee!"

By the time Saturday came around, Lily had
already had three play rehearsals, and loved
every minute of them. The story of the play

was of the Christmas Angel watching over the world in December, and seeing a family who were constantly arguing. Over the course of the play, the Christmas Angel reminded the family of the true meaning of Christmas, and inspired them to be kinder to each other. There were lots of songs to learn as well as her lines, but Lily was enjoying herself hugely.

The only problem was that Buster seemed to be behaving extra badly in Lily's absence. Mum had caught him sharpening his claws on the table leg, which had left scratch marks in the wood. He'd knocked over a lamp in the living room by pouncing on the tassels that dangled so temptingly from the lampshade, and he'd actually lashed out at Jessica when she'd pulled him off the sofa by his tail. Jessica had howled with shock, apparently, and had a long red scratch on her arm to show for the encounter.

"Thank goodness it's the weekend now and I can keep an eye on you," Lily told Buster, trying on her angel costume in her bedroom. She beamed at her reflection. Mrs Cookson, the teacher who was making the costumes for the play, had given Lily her outfit the day before at school. It was gorgeous! The dress was silver and sparkly, and covered with sequins, and she also had the most wonderful glittering gauzy wings edged with long white feathers.

Buster eyed Lily's wings with interest as she fastened them to her back, and stared as she pretended to fly around the room. "Silly billy, do you think I'm a bird?" Lily laughed, when he chased after her.

"Lily!" called Mum just then from downstairs. "Can you watch Jessica for a minute while I sort this laundry?"

"Sure," Lily shouted back. She took off the dress and wings, and laid them carefully on her bed. The Kitten Club meeting was at her house today and she couldn't wait to show her friends.

She grabbed Buster and took him down to the living room where Jessica was sitting on the carpet, surrounded by toys. She was playing with some stacking rings, and every time she put a ring on to the central pole, Lily would cheer and clap and do a little dance. Jessica thought this was the funniest thing ever and got more and more excited, laughing even before she'd put a ring on to the pole in anticipation of Lily doing the dance. Meanwhile, Buster was careering around the room after a pink squeaky ball.

Lily loved making Jessica laugh and started thinking of other ways to amuse her. She put the stacking rings on to her head then wobbled her head around until they plopped off, one by one. Jessica squealed and clapped at the sight. Then Lily juggled with Jessica's squishy beanbags, pulling funny faces and pretending to fall over as she caught them. Jessica nearly fell over herself from laughing so much.

Jessica wasn't the only one who was watching Lily's antics now. Buster was fascinated by the flying beanbags too and sat staring at them, his little eyes tracking their movement. Then, as Lily threw one of the beanbags too far, Buster went sprinting after it and pounced on it. Jessica thought this was hilarious and laughed even harder.

Pleased that Buster wanted to join in the game, Lily started throwing the beanbags for him to pounce on. She was laughing so hard herself that her throws became wilder and wilder – and one beanbag flew right up on to the mantelpiece where it just missed a glass vase. Buster didn't hesitate. He leaped on to the bookcase, and then on to the mantelpiece. But the mantelpiece was an old marble one that was slippery under his feet … and he skidded right along it, knocking everything off as he went!

Lily gasped in horror as the vase fell off and smashed, the framed photos of Lily and Jessica toppled over with a horrible shattering sound, and Mum's favourite stone paperweight in the shape of an eagle fell off and cracked clean in two.

Jessica burst into shocked tears. "Oh no," muttered Lily. Buster, sensing a telling-off, hurtled down from the mantelpiece at once, his ears flattened in alarm.

"What on earth was that?" cried Mum, hurrying through from the kitchen, just in time to see Buster streak out of the room and upstairs. She put a hand up to her mouth and looked as if she might cry when she saw all the breakages.

"I'm sorry, Mum, it was my fault," Lily said. She felt awful.

"All my lovely things," said Mum. "That cat, honestly – he's more trouble than he's worth!"

Chapter 5

Half an hour later, when everything had been cleaned up, the doorbell rang. It was time for Kitten Club! As her friends arrived, Lily led them through to the kitchen where she'd set out a plate of mince pies and some glasses of lemonade. She couldn't relax properly for the first few minutes though. All she could think of was

Mum saying that Buster was more trouble than he was worth. She'd said it as if she really hated him!

"Are you OK, Lily?" Molly asked, nudging her after a while. "You're very quiet."

"Yeah, that's not like you, Lils," Ella put in, leaning forward. "What's up? And where's Buster anyway?"

Lily sighed. "Hiding upstairs from Mum, probably," she said. "He's in *huuuge* trouble right now." She went on to explain what had just happened.

"All kittens break stuff," Amy said kindly. "They can't help it. Ginger knocked over a pot plant in the garden last week, and the pot smashed. It was only an accident so we couldn't be too cross."

"I know, but the problem is, Buster just

keeps doing these things," Lily replied. "Like, he's wrecked the furniture and Mum's pyjamas, and smashed her vase and paperweight... She's getting really fed up with him. Today she even said she thought he was more trouble than he was worth – like she'd rather not have him at all!"

Everyone went quiet at this. "People say things like that when they're cross but they don't always mean it," Ruby said.

Lily shrugged. "You didn't see her face," she said gloomily. "She was like this—" And Lily pulled the most shocked, horrified, furious expression she could muster up, which made the others laugh.

"You are so going to be an actress, Lily," Mia said, spluttering on her lemonade. "Hey, that reminds me, how did your audition go?"

Lily smiled for what felt like the first time in ages. "I got the part!" she said. "I'm the Christmas Angel. Oh, and wait till you see my dress – it's amazing." She stood up, remembering it was upstairs on her bed. "Actually … why don't you come and have a look? We can see what Buster's up to as well – make sure he's not causing any more trouble."

The girls followed Lily upstairs. As she reached her bedroom, she pushed open the door and said, "Ta-dah!" But the smile vanished from her face as she realized that Buster was on her bed, having some kind of fight with her dress. The wings were ripped, sequins and feathers had been torn off, and he was kicking and chewing at the neckline. It was ruined!

Lily let out a scream. "Buster! Oh, Buster, how could you?" she wailed.

Buster, realizing he was in trouble again, leaped off the bed in a panic, feathers

floating after him, and scurried out of the room, almost tripping over in his haste to get away.

The girls crowded in to inspect the damage. "It's completely wrecked," Lily said, bursting into tears. "Mrs Cookson's going to go nuts when she sees it. And what will Mum say?"

"What will Mum say about what?" came a voice. Then Lily's mum gasped as she saw what had happened. "Oh, no. Your dress!"

Tears rolled down Lily's face. "I must have left my bedroom door open earlier," she said miserably. "It's all my fault – again!"

Ella and Ruby, who were closest to Lily, both put an arm round her and tried to comfort her. It was awful seeing bubbly Lily so miserable. "We can fix it," Ruby said, handing her friend a tissue. "My mum's brilliant with a sewing machine. I bet she wouldn't mind repairing the wings."

"We can stick the feathers back on too,"
Molly put in. "My dad's got some superglue
– I'm sure he'll help us."

"I'll see if I can patch up the dress later,"
Mum sighed, looking thoroughly fed up. "I've
got to give Jessica her milk now, though."

Lily's mum left the room and the girls
crowded round Lily.

"Don't worry, we'll sort it out," Amy
said, picking up some of the feathers.

Lily blew her nose and gave her friends
a watery smile. "Thanks, guys," she said.
"I shouldn't have shouted at Buster like that
– he didn't know it was my special costume.
I should have hung it up somewhere safe
where he couldn't reach it, and shut my
door, but I forgot. It's—"

She broke off as they heard Lily's mum

scolding Buster downstairs. "No! Naughty! Claws OFF, Buster. Honestly! If I'd known just how much trouble you were going to be, I'd never have let Lily get you in the first place."

Lily's mouth dropped open in horror and she looked as if she was about to cry again. "Did you hear that?" she gulped. "I've got to make Buster behave better. What if Mum decides she's had enough of his naughty tricks and wants to give him away?"

"She won't," Molly said immediately, helping Amy pick up the last few feathers. "No way. Your mum wouldn't do that."

"But she just said she wishes we'd never got him," Lily sniffled. Her tummy ached at the thought of not having Buster. She couldn't bear to even imagine it. "He keeps

breaking things and scratching the furniture
– he's driving her mad."

"Maybe Buster needs a scratching post
to stop him sharpening his
claws on everything
else," Mia suggested.
"You can buy them in
pet shops. While it's
cold and rainy and the
kittens don't want to go
outside, it might be good
to have one in the house."

"Dad was talking about helping me
make one," Ella put in. "Hey, I know!
Why don't I ask if he'll help us all make
scratching posts for the kittens next
time we have a Kitten Club meeting
at our house?"

"Brilliant idea," Ruby said. "And we could give them to the kittens as Christmas presents!"

Everyone liked the sound of that – especially Lily. "I need to try harder too," she said, rubbing her red eyes with the tissue. "I have to remember to close the bedroom and bathroom doors, and get him to play outside more often." She gave her friends a watery smile. "In fact, why don't we take him into the garden now? Come on. We can give him his first Kitten Training lesson."

Chapter 6

The girls wrapped up in their coats and scarves and took Buster into the garden. "A scratching post is a great idea," Lily said, "but I'm not sure I can wait until Christmas. Let's see if we can teach him to sharpen his claws outside for now – on tree trunks or on the fence or … well, on anything, as long as it isn't furniture!"

They walked over to the cherry tree and Lily crouched down in front of it, still holding her kitten. "Here we are," she said. "Now, this is what you need to do…" She put Buster's front paws on the tree in the perfect trunk-scratching position. But Buster wriggled out of her grasp and went off to sniff a nearby stone.

"Buster! Pay attention," Molly said.

"Watch me, Buster," Lily said. She put her hands on the trunk, pretending to be a cat as she scraped her fingers down the bark. "See? Easy. Now it's your turn."

Again, she picked him up and set his front paws against the bark. "Sharpen your claws," she told him. "Go on!"

"Much better than furniture," Mia said encouragingly. "Give it a try, Buster."

But either Buster didn't understand or he just wasn't interested in doing what he was told. He scampered off to pounce on some long blades of grass which were blowing in the wind instead.

Lily sighed. "We'll try again tomorrow," she said, feeling a little downcast. "But really, Buster, you've got to get the hang of it. You need to get yourself back into Mum's good books, otherwise…" She winced, not wanting to think about what might happen. Her mum's words about wishing she'd never agreed to a kitten kept running round her head. Lily had to help him become better behaved.

Just then Buster did a flying leap right into the rosemary plant and started chewing its stems. Lily groaned and clapped a hand to her head. "It'll take more than a quick lesson in the garden to stop his crazy behaviour, that's for sure," she sighed.

The girls played with Buster outside for a while longer. Ella suggested that lots of outdoor play might tire him out, so that he'd sleep more indoors and wouldn't have time to cause trouble. "Good thinking," Lily said and shivered. "Brrrr. Let's go in now though and warm up. I'm cold!"

Lily's mum had left out some art things for the girls – different-coloured paper, pens,

pencils, glitter and glue – and they sat round
the kitchen table with mugs of hot chocolate,
making Christmas cards for their kittens. Lily
drew a picture of herself as the Christmas

Angel next to Buster with a
matching silver halo above
his head. "I'll help him to
be a little angel from now
on," she vowed, adding smiles
to both their faces. She glanced

over at Buster who was now fast asleep in his
basket, worn out after his outdoor
adventures, just as Ella had predicted.

"He looks so adorable when he's asleep,"
Amy said, seeing Lily gazing at him.

Lily smiled. "Doesn't he? Good as gold.
You'd never guess it was the same kitten
who wrecked my dress earlier."

"Talking of which…" Lily's mum said, coming into the room just then. She was carrying the remains of Lily's costume as well as a bridesmaid dress Lily had worn the previous summer, which was now a bit small for her. "I think I'll be able to repair your angel dress using the fabric from this," she said. "Will that be all right?"

Lily was so relieved that her mum didn't sound cross any more that she ran over and hugged her. "Thanks, Mum," she said. "That sounds brilliant."

During the next week, the rehearsals for the Christmas play took place every day after school. Lily was really enjoying learning her role, apart from the fact that she saw less of Buster. Unfortunately, this meant less time for her Kitten Training and her plans to tire him out in the garden, especially as it was dark by the time she got home.

Meanwhile, Buster seemed to be getting naughtier and naughtier. On Monday, he jumped on to the breakfast table and knocked Lily's glass of milk over. On Tuesday, he clawed great scratches in the side of the sofa. And on Wednesday, he chewed through the electric cable of a lamp, dug all the soil out of one of the house plants and bit Jessica when she pulled his tail!

By Thursday, Lily was dreading going home to see what awful things Buster had got up to, and found it really hard to concentrate on the play rehearsal. Mum had looked utterly exasperated with Buster's antics the night before and Lily was more convinced than ever that she was having second thoughts about having such a naughty pet.

After the rehearsal that evening, one of Lily's friend's mums gave her a lift home. As soon as she got in the house, she pulled her coat off and called Buster's name.

"Ahh," her mum said. "Lily – I need to talk to you about Buster…"

But Lily was already in the kitchen, and

stopped dead as she saw that Buster's food bowl and cat bed had vanished. *I need to talk to you about Buster,* Mum had said, and immediately Lily feared the worst.

Surely … surely Mum hadn't already got rid of him?

Chapter 7

Lily couldn't help herself. She burst into floods of tears at the thought of never seeing her funny, adorable kitten again. This was going to be the worst Christmas ever! Why hadn't she tried harder to train him? Why hadn't she done a better job of keeping him amused so that he wouldn't do naughty things? This was all her fault!

"Lily, whatever's the matter?" her mum said, coming into the kitchen just then and finding Lily in a sobbing heap on the floor.

"Oh, Mum, why did you have to give Buster away?" Lily wailed. "I never even got to say goodbye!"

"Lily McCarthy, what are you talking about?" Mum asked, crouching beside her and putting an arm round her. "Buster hasn't gone anywhere, he's fast asleep on the sofa."

Lily sniffed and stared at Mum. "He's ... on the sofa?" she hiccuped. "You haven't given him away?"

"Of course I haven't given him away,"

Mum exclaimed, ruffling Lily's hair. "I wouldn't dream of it! Yes, he's been a bit of a pest recently, but he's only a kitten. He'll be more sensible when he's older." She chuckled. "Just like you and Jessica. Believe me, Lils, you were much more trouble than any kitten when you were a toddler. But it never crossed my mind to give *you* to anyone else."

Lily blew her nose and dabbed at her eyes. "When I couldn't see Buster's things, I just thought…" she said, relief flooding through her. "After you were so cross with him this morning, I've been so worried. I thought you didn't want us to have a kitten any more."

Her mum hugged her. "Buster's bowl is in the dishwasher," she said. "And his bed is in the utility room where I gave it a wash earlier.

I know I've been a bit bad-tempered lately, but it's just because I'm tired. That's what I was going to say when you came in – that I'm sorry for being grumpy with you and Buster. As soon as Jessica gets her new tooth through, we should all sleep better, and I won't feel so frazzled." She kissed the top of Lily's head. "So you dry your eyes now and go and give that kitten of yours a big cuddle, because he's not going anywhere, OK?"

Lily nodded, feeling much better. "Thanks, Mum," she said. "You're the best mum ever."

The next Saturday, the Kitten Club meeting was at Ella's house. True to her word, she'd asked her dad if they could make kitten

scratching posts and he'd gathered some
short planks of wood, and a roll of sisal –
thin, hairy rope – that they could use.

Ella's dad cut lengths of sisal for them
and nailed one end of each piece to the tops
of their wooden boards.

"Now you need to wind the rope round and round, keeping the loops tightly together," he told them. "When you're done, I'll nail the other end down too, and then we'll attached the boards to their bases."

The girls began winding the rough rope round their pieces of wood. Once they'd finished, and Ella's dad had nailed each rope-end in place and fastened the boards to their wooden bases, Ella's mum produced a pot of ribbons and plastic baubles and suggested that the girls attach some to the top of the scratching posts. "As well as making them look pretty, it'll encourage the kittens to reach up and grab them – and hopefully they'll quickly learn that the rope is really good to sharpen their claws on," she said.

"Or you can tie catnip toys to the top," Ella's dad suggested. "They love the smell of that."

The girls chatted while they made their posts. "This is going to be Buster's new year's resolution," Lily decided. "To learn to use his scratching post so that he stops sharpening his claws on the furniture."

"Truffle's resolution should be to grow up into a big brave cat, who doesn't put up with any nonsense from my brothers or dog," Molly laughed. "Although she is getting a bit feistier already. The other day my brother Luke was playing a really noisy game on the PlayStation and Truffle managed to turn off the TV by jumping on to the remote. It was so funny! It was just an accident, but you should have seen

Luke's face. The Kitten Strikes Back!"

"Honey's resolution is to chill out a bit," Ella said, tying a long silver ribbon with a jingling bell on the end to her scratching post. But the moment the words were out of her mouth, she let out a shriek as Honey suddenly came flying through the air on to her lap, making everyone jump.

The girls all laughed. "I think Honey's got other ideas about your resolution," Ruby chuckled. "She's planning to have lots more fun. Chilling out is boring, right, Honey?"

"I can't wait for Christmas," Amy said, putting the finishing touches to her scratching post. "I'm going to hang up a stocking for Ginger, just in case 'Santa Paws' pops in with some little treats."

"Great idea," Lily said. "Ooh, and talking of Christmas, I've got you all tickets to see me in my school play next Friday night. Mum said we could have a little party back at our house afterwards with hot chocolate and Yule log."

"And can we get your autograph for when you're really famous?" Molly joked. "We can tell everyone that we saw you in your first starring role!"

Lily struck a dramatic pose, and the others laughed. Then Honey leaped on to the table and skidded right through a tangle of ribbons. "Oh, Honey," Ella giggled, unravelling the wild-eyed kitten. "Were you trying to wrap yourself up as an early present? You'd be the best Christmas present ever!"

Once Lily was home that afternoon, she decided that she'd give Buster his Christmas present early. There was no time to lose!

She already knew he loved the smell of catnip as he had a catnip mouse that he often played with, so she tied its tail on to one of the ribbons at the top of the scratching post. Then she put it down on the kitchen floor and brought him over to show him his new present.

Buster was intrigued by the ribbons and toys at the top of the post and reached up his soft paws to get them. Lily could see his

little black nose twitching too as he smelled the catnip. And then, as his claws caught in the rope, he pulled his paw free and began scratching in earnest at it.

"Oh, good boy, Buster," Lily said, stroking him.

Buster immediately froze and looked guilty – as if he thought Lily was about to tell him off for sharpening his claws.

Lily smiled. "You carry on scratching, mister," she told him, tickling him under the chin until he began to purr. "This is the one place in the whole house that you're allowed to sharpen your claws, OK?"

Buster purred even louder, and Lily felt like purring too when he went on scratching at the sisal-covered post for several minutes. "There, doesn't that feel nice?" she cooed, stroking him happily. "Now we just need you to stop climbing shelves and knocking things off and doing all your other tricks," she went on. "And everything will be perfect. OK?"

Chapter 8

The next week seemed to fly by. The good news was that the weather was much brighter, so Buster spent lots of the day outside and less time indoors wrecking the house, according to Mum. He'd also got the hang of his scratching post and loved sharpening his claws on it.

The bad news was that Lily's dad still

wasn't sure if he'd be back from Scotland in time to see the play. "I'm sorry, love," he said on the phone the night before the show. "I'll do my best to get there and see you but I just can't promise."

"Don't worry, Dad, I understand," Lily managed to say, although there was a big lump in her throat. She was gladder than ever that her Kitten Club friends would be in the audience to watch her.

The next day, Lily had butterflies in her tummy like never before. They'd had a dress rehearsal that morning in front of the rest of the school and all sorts of things had gone wrong – one of the children who was dressed up as a Christmas tree had tripped over and hurt herself onstage, the Snowman had forgotten his words and the baby Jesus doll had fallen out of the crib with a loud clatter. Worst of all, when Lily came to say her first lines, her mind went completely blank. "Good evening to you all," she heard Mrs Matthews whisper from the side of the stage, and then the words fell back into her head, thankfully. "Good evening to you all," she repeated. "I am the Christmas Angel, come to Earth…"

"Oh dear," one of the Year 6 girls had said once the curtain had fallen and the dress rehearsal was over. "That didn't go very well."

Mrs Matthews didn't look too concerned. "That's what dress rehearsals are for, though," she said confidently.

"You'll see. It'll be all right on the night."

When the time came to put on her costume that evening, Lily could hardly pull up her silver tights because her hands were shaking so much. Luckily, Mum had been able to repair her dress pretty well with the extra bridesmaid dress fabric, and the wings had been patched up too. Once she was dressed and in her wings and halo, Mrs Matthews patted on some sparkly face powder with a powder puff, and added a few silver sprinkles above her eyes. She was ready!

Backstage, Lily and the other actors could hear the school hall filling up with parents and friends. Some of the performers were getting giddy with nerves while others wanted to sit very still on their own. Lily's heart was pounding, she needed the loo and her hands felt clammy. Oh, why had she put herself forward for the Christmas Angel? She was going to forget all her words again and make a complete idiot of herself! She wished she could be safely at home with Buster right now.

"Special delivery for Lily McCarthy," came a voice just then, and Lily swung round in delight. She'd recognize that voice anywhere – her dad! She flung her arms round him and hugged him so tightly she could hardly breathe.

"You made it!" she cried happily. "Oh, Dad, I've really missed you!"

He hugged her back, and she felt safe and warm in his arms, as if nothing could go wrong. "I've missed you too, love," he said. "I'm so glad I made it home in time to see the show. Oh, and your friends wanted me to deliver this to you."

He gave her a hand-made card with a black cat on the front. The words GOOD LUCK! were written above it, in Molly's handwriting. Smiling, Lily opened the card to see good luck messages from all the Kitten Club girls – and even some paw-prints as if Buster was wishing her luck too. Seeing her dad and the card made her feel a hundred times better. All of a sudden, she couldn't wait to get onstage.

"Is everyone ready?" Mrs Matthews called just then, bustling into the backstage area. She raised her eyebrows at the sight of Lily's dad there. "Would you mind taking your seat now, Mr McCarthy? The show's about to begin."

"Sure," he said, giving Lily's hand a last squeeze. "Good luck, Lils. See you later!"

"Bye, Dad." Lily smiled.

Suddenly, the hall went quiet. "Good evening, ladies and gentlemen, boys and girls," she heard the headteacher, Mr Holmes, say. "Welcome to our school. We are proud to present to you our Christmas play, called *The Christmas Angel*."

Lily could hear the audience clapping,

and an icy chill trickled down her back. She took a deep breath and walked out on to the stage, her heart pounding. This was it – her big moment in the spotlight!

"You were awesome, Lily," Molly said, biting into a slice of Yule log and licking her chocolatey fingers. "Just the best person in the whole play."

"Really?" Lily blushed. "Honestly?"

"Really, honestly, truly," Molly assured her. "You rocked!"

"She's right," Lily's dad said, hugging her again. "You stole the show. I'm so proud of you."

"What a star," Mum agreed, with a wink. "You were wonderful."

Lily and the other Kitten Club girls were back at Lily's house with steaming mugs of hot chocolate and whipped cream, and thick slabs of squidgy Yule log. The Christmas show had been amazing, even if Lily said so herself. She had loved being onstage and seeing her friends and family smiling back at her from the audience. And the roar of applause that had come at the end … it gave her goosebumps every time she thought about it.

"I can't believe it's all over," Lily said now, sipping her hot chocolate. "And next we've got Christmas to look forward to!"

Her eye was caught by the Christmas tree in the corner of the room, which she and her mum had decorated with tinsel, baubles and fairy lights a few evenings earlier.

They'd decided to make it kitten-proof and
baby-proof by not hanging anything on low
branches so that neither Jessica nor Buster
would be tempted to pull the decorations
straight off again.

"What does Buster think of your tree?"
Ruby asked, seeing Lily
looking at it. "Ziggy
loves the fairy lights
on ours. We've got
the sort that flash on
and off and he
spends ages just staring
up at them in a trance."

"Buster's been pretty cool," Lily said.
"He likes playing with the lower branches,
jumping up and batting them, but that's about
it. I think he might be growing up at last,

you know. He's definitely calmed down lately."

As if he'd heard the girls talking about him, Buster chose that very minute to scamper into the room. His ears were back and he had a wild look in his eyes as if he was in a mischievous mood. "Uh-oh, you spoke too soon," Ella laughed. "He's all skittish tonight. Getting excited about Christmas, are you, Buster?"

Buster certainly did seem excited about something. Lily took a piece of tinsel off the tree and pulled it around the room, and he chased after it at full pelt. Then he looked up at the Christmas tree and seemed to notice all the other decorations and tinsel on the higher branches. And before anyone could stop him, he'd leaped on to the mantelpiece and then made a mighty spring from there to the top branches of the tree.

"Buster! Oh, Buster, what are you doing?" Lily cried, clapping a hand to her mouth.

Buster wrestled with a piece of tinsel and sent a shiny red bauble flying off its branch as he clambered frantically up the tree. Then as he got higher up, he managed to knock the gold cardboard star off the top branch, sending it plunging to the ground.

"He says he's the only Christmas star in this house, thank you very much," Molly chuckled. "Oh, Buster, trust you!"

Lily was laughing so much she could hardly stand up straight. "Come here, you cheeky boy," she said, reaching up and pulling Buster out of the tree. "What are you like? Just as I was telling the others how calm you are too!"

Buster purred in her arms, his green eyes reflecting the twinkling fairy lights, and Lily laughed again and held him tight. "You are my Christmas star, Buster, don't worry," she told him. "And I just know all six of us girls and our purr-fect pets are going to have a very happy mew year!"

Collect all the books
in the series!

Ginger's New Home

Smokey's Great Escape

Ziggy's Big Adventure

Hodge's New Friend

Truffle's Secret Hideaway